# Snow

This Faber book belongs to

......................................................

*To my family, friends and teachers who*
*always encouraged me to do what I love*
*C.R.*

First published in the UK in 2014
by Faber and Faber Ltd,
Bloomsbury House,
74–77 Great Russell Street, London WC1B 3DA

The text was first published as the poem 'Snow' in
Walter de la Mare's *Peacock Pie* poetry collection in 1924.

Printed in China

Text © The Literary Trustees of Walter de la Mare, 1969
Illustrations © Carolina Rabei, 2014

A CIP record for this book is available
from the British Library

HB ISBN 978–0–571–31219–1
PB ISBN 978–0–571–30557–5

10 9 8 7 6 5 4 3 2

FSC
www.fsc.org

MIX
Paper from
responsible sources
FSC® C020056

A FABER PICTURE BOOK

# Snow

### Walter de la Mare

#### Illustrated by Carolina Rabei

ff

FABER & FABER

No breath of wind,
No gleam of sun—

Still the white snow
Whirls softly down—

Twig and bough
And blade and thorn
All in an icy
Quiet, forlorn.

Whispering, rustling,
Through the air,
On sill and stone,
Roof – everywhere,

It heaps its powdery
Crystal flakes,

Of every tree
A mountain makes;

Till pale and faint
At shut of day,
Stoops from the West
One wintry ray.

And, feathered in fire,
Where ghosts the moon,
A robin shrills
His lonely tune.